Return to the Wild

Story by Mary Busby

Illustrations by Emily Wikle

Print ISBN: 978-0-9968462-2-6
Digital ISBN: 978-0-9968462-3-3

First Edition

For our grandson, Ashton

Also by Mary Busby:
The Cat Tamer

I know the sound of the waves
I hope for the warmth of the sun.
All my life I have gathered them
Now let us fly free with the breeze.

CHAPTER ONE

“Hello, Mr. Barlow!” Brianna charged up the driveway to greet her friend.

“Hello, Brianna.”

She reached down to pet Kitty Girl, and the cat’s loud purring made Mr. Barlow laugh.

“She’s missed your visits,” he said. “Are you home for the rest of the summer?”

Brianna nodded.

“Good! You are in luck today because Joey and I are going to visit baby barn owls whose nest was smashed. I know there’s an adventure waiting for you. Would you like to join us?”

"Baby barn owls! I hope they're OK." Brianna looked up at Mr. Barlow. "I've never seen one. What do they look like?"

"As chicks they look like baby dinosaurs with big beaks and large feet called talons." Mr. Barlow held his hand out like a claw. "While they mature, the area around their eyes grows feathers in a heart shape, so they have a whimsical look. Their beaks look smaller because the downy fluff turns into beautiful spotted and decorated feathers. They hunt at night and silently grab the mice, voles, and rats who eat at night too. Because our neighborhood is so wooded, we see the great horned owls more often than the barn owls, who hunt in the open."

Brianna looked around her at all of Mr. Barlow's trees, bushes, flowers, and vines. His yard was a secret garden, and she felt very special to have such a nice man for her neighbor and friend. She liked petting his cats and helping him with his gardening. She couldn't believe that at one time she had thought that he was really strange, just because no one on their street ever saw him. The kids told stories that he made potions and talked to himself. But when Joey was riding by his house and heard him talking, Mr. Barlow was actually talking to his cats, especially Kitty Girl, whom he was trying to feed and take care of since she had been abandoned. After spying on Mr. Barlow and then finally meeting him, Brianna learned he was a nice man who did nice things for people and animals.

"This is so much more fun than camp!" Brianna said.

***

"Joey, move over. There's no room for me." Brianna scooted onto the rough, torn vinyl seat. She carefully untangled the faded seatbelts.

Growling like an old man, the engine of Mr. Barlow's truck started.

Joey turned to Brianna. "Hey, it's great you're going with us. Maybe the barn owls will swoop down and grab you and take you back to their nest!"

Shaking her head at his silliness, Brianna again thought of all the mean things Joey had said about Mr. Barlow in the past. Joey had told her that Mr. Barlow was a magician with special powers. That scared her a little at the time. She smiled as she remembered the way Mr. Barlow talked to his cats as if they were children. Over time, she and Joey had learned that their neighbor was a gentle man with a big heart. He taught them his woodworking skills and let them help him build his birdhouses.

Brianna glanced behind her and saw a big cardboard box strapped in the truck bed. Since it seemed out of place, she asked what it was for.

Mr. Barlow looked for traffic before pulling out of his driveway. "The box is a good way to safely transport the baby barn owls from the smashed nest at Tom's ranch to my house."

"Who's Tom?"

"Tom Wilson is an old friend of mine."

Brianna realized that she knew very little about Mr. Barlow's past.

"He lived down the road from my house when I was growing up. We hung out a lot."

"What did you do?" Brianna asked.

"He taught me how to ride horses, how to survive in the wilderness, and how to herd cattle. His family owns one of the largest surviving ranches in the entire valley. We shared a lot of exciting adventures together, and he knows how much I love animals. That's why he called me rather than someone else to save these baby barn owls."

"What happened to them?" Brianna asked.

"An earthquake caused an old oak to drop a branch that held the nest. The nest split apart, and it was so smashed that the babies will need a new nest in the tree. The parents won't feed the chicks on the ground, and the chicks really need their parents to survive."

"What do you mean—they need their parents?" Joey asked.

"These chicks are still being fed by their parents because they're so young and helpless. Each one needs to eat several mice every day. That's why Tom needs my help. I can make a sturdy wood box big enough to fit all seven baby chicks. Hopefully, we can place the box back into the tree and the parents will continue to feed the chicks until they are old enough to leave the nest."

Brianna imagined all the babies in a big soft nest, crying for their food and sleeping peacefully after they were fed. Maybe I can keep one, she thought.

She turned to Mr. Barlow. "Is Mr. Wilson still herding cattle?" she asked. She had seen round-ups in movies.

"You'll see." Mr. Barlow pointed to the trees and open pasture land they passed. "Tom and I grew up in this large valley where all the ranchers raised cattle and horses on big pieces of property. Long ago, these ranches were self-sufficient, and big families lived and worked together to make a ranch thrive."

"Did you live on a cattle ranch?" Joey asked.

"No, but I lived near several of them where my friends invited me to ride horses and dirt bikes, and for several summers I worked on those cattle ranches cutting trees, mending fences, and rounding up cattle."

"Wow, that must have been hard work," Joey said.

"It was hot and very physical work, but I loved it." Mr. Barlow let out a sigh. "The stillness of the meadows and the sound of birds made me happy. That's when I knew I wanted to live on a big piece of property and grow things and build birdhouses." He pointed to the side of the road. "These are the native trees that the indigenous tribes used for food when they harvested the oak acorns. The black oaks have larger acorns, which taste better, but they grow farther from the ocean. The Ohlone Tribe depended on the trees for their main food source. Imagine eating an oak cake without sugar or butter for your daily meal all your life."

"What? No McDonald's?" Joey exclaimed.

Brianna shook her head again and looked out at the pale grasses and clustered bright green oaks. She wondered if the natives had walked on this trail, which was now asphalt.

Mr. Barlow turned the truck off the highway to face a long metal gate that blocked their passage down a dirt road. "Here we are. One of the last surviving ranches of the past." Overhead, a wooden sign read *Rancho Los Lobos.* After opening and carefully closing the gate, Mr. Barlow drove on. Low, round hills studded with dark-green trees rose on both sides of the road. Gradually the land flattened out, and small groups of cattle grazed. Brianna had never visited a real cattle ranch before, and she could feel the wildness in the soft air. She stuck her head out the window, taking in the sweet smells of oat and wheat.

Suddenly a large group of buildings appeared before them like a small village. Big machines were parked under even bigger sheds. Rusted cars and tractor parts lined the side of the road, heaped together with broken chairs and other neglected household goods. White wooden fences crisscrossed the land everywhere, penning in horses and cattle that shook their heads and swished their tails to discourage the flies from landing on them. Large multi-colored chickens and a rooster pecked quickly, darting their heads back and forth over the dusty ground. Barking dogs raced toward the truck and bared their scary-looking teeth. Brianna shrank back from the window and waited for Mr. Barlow to do something.

A tall, thin man in blue-jean overalls and rubber boots waved the dogs away. "Hush up!" he said.

Mr. Barlow opened his door and stepped out to shake hands with the tanned, black-haired man with the loud voice. "You look good, Tom. It's great to see you again after all these years."

"It's good to see you, too. It's been too long. The folks aren't getting any younger, and me and Sis are doing more and more of the work, but we sold 500 head of good beef cattle last year, and we hope to do more this year."

"How many horses have you raised?"

"Just enough to run the ranch."

"Well, Tom, you're the best rancher around here, and I'm so glad that you called me to help with the owls."

"To tell the truth, John, I didn't know who else to call. Your gettin' on with the animals has always been your strong suit." Mr. Barlow's friend gestured toward Joey and Brianna. "Who are these fine-looking young people?"

"Brianna and Joey, this is Mr. Wilson, an old friend. Tom, these are my favorite neighbors."

Brianna and Joey shook hands with Mr. Wilson.

"Why are your hands so rough?" Brianna asked.

Mr. Wilson chuckled. "I like to work with them. Here in this beautiful valley, not many ranches still exist and breed cattle and horses. I'm proud of the fact that our family has survived and thrived for generations on this one rancho. I can trace my family back many generations, even to when the Spanish owned this land."

Mr. Wilson smiled and motioned toward the meadow behind him. "Come on over, and I'll show you where the tree branch went down," he said. "The babies are still on the ground, and the mom and dad are flying around and looking down, but they're not feeding the babies. I can understand their fear. This is not what they know, and the chicks are calling for help, but we're here, so that's why the parents won't drop to the ground. It makes them too vulnerable to predators. Even though they are connected with their chicks, the parents fear attackers. These birds have a strong sense of survival."

Mr. Wilson led the small group up a hill and down a steep incline. On the left, an enormous bare oak branch lay on the ground next to an old oak that was barely clinging to life after having survived many decades of wind and rain and drought. Brianna looked up at the sky and imagined what the old oak had looked like as a healthy and life-giving tree. She understood that the barn owls had chosen this tree, even though it was old, because it was solid–until now.

"Mr. Wilson, how long has this oak tree been here?" she asked.

"It must be at least 100 years old. My grandmother said that she and her brothers would climb the branches and use them as their lookouts to keep an eye out for Indians and rustlers."

Forgetting about the owlets on the ground for a moment, Brianna said, "This tree is like a part of your family. Why did it fall?"

"The family was at dinner. I live here with my folks and sister, and we all felt the earthquake shudder. Then we heard the cracking of the branch as it split off from the tree."

Brianna couldn't see the nest from where she stood, but then she heard hissing and walked around the branch. There, in a large pile of sticks, leaves, and grass, seven baby dinosaurs with yellow-white fluff reared back and showed their long, scary feet with narrow, sharp claws. One of them was bloody and still. She wanted to move closer, but she felt helpless, so she waited for Mr. Wilson or Mr. Barlow to do something.

Leaning over to examine the chicks, Mr. Barlow asked, "How long have they been here, Tom? On the ground, I mean."

"Just a few hours. They can survive maybe a couple days, but I didn't want them to starve, so I thought you might take them home, feed them, and then we can decide what to do once they're stronger and over their shock."

"Why do they rear back like that and stick up their feet at us?" Brianna asked.

"They're trying to protect themselves," Mr. Wilson said. "So they put up their feet first, their strongest weapon. They use their talons or claws to grab their prey, kill it, and hold it while they eat it."

"What about those horrible beaks?" Brianna asked.

Mr. Wilson chuckled. "Their bodies will change dramatically in the next several weeks. The first thing to worry about is their food source." He looked at Mr. Barlow. "So, what do you think, John?"

Mr. Barlow carefully examined the chicks. "It's going to be tough," he said. "I'm not sure the smallest one will make it. He's only about four inches tall, and some of his big brothers and sisters are nearly eight inches. Feeding each little beak will be tricky. I don't know."

"Please, you have to help them," Brianna begged. "You're the cat tamer. You can tame anything."

"Thank you for your faith in me, Brianna, but I know very little about barn owls and their feeding habits. Hungry, abandoned cats are one thing. These are wild creatures of the night. But I do have a friend who helps raise baby condors in a sanctuary down the coast not far from here. She may know the right food and treatment for these little ones. I guess the least I can do is try and see what happens. They'll starve to death if we leave them here. The parents will never get over their fear of us and come down and feed them."

Brianna remembered when she had first seen Kitty Girl and how afraid the animal was of her. Then Mr. Barlow—through kindness and patience—tamed the cat and made it a friend. Brianna had seen for herself the special power Mr. Barlow possessed with animals. He was not a magician, as Joey had thought, but they had seen him change frightened, starving cats into good friends, and they had watched him create birdhouses out of raw wood and turn them into safe shelters.

CHAPTER TWO

Mr. Barlow returned to the nest site with his box filled with wood shavings. He gently lifted each chick, holding them by their backs, and then carefully closed the box flaps so the chicks were in the dark. They screeched and hissed, and Brianna and Joey whispered to each other that they sounded just like snakes.

After carefully strapping the box into the truck bed, Mr. Barlow and Mr. Wilson spent several minutes catching up on the news about Mr. Wilson's family. Then Mr. Wilson turned to Brianna and Joey. "Would you two like a tour of the ranch on an ATV when you bring the chicks back?" he asked. "I think you might enjoy seeing a cattle round-up from a big, fast go-cart."

Joey immediately answered, "You mean ride a real quad with giant wheels?"

"That's right. I couldn't show you all 2,000 acres, but we could watch our cowboys round up the Holsteins on the north range and follow them into the corrals."

Brianna imagined herself as an Indian princess riding her favorite pinto bareback across the plains, following the buffalo as she looked over the wide-open meadows.

"I have two side-by-sides," Mr. Wilson said, smiling at Mr. Barlow. "So I can fit me and Joey in one ATV, and you and Brianna can ride in the other one. You still remember how to drive an ATV, right, John?

Mr. Barlow laughed. "I'm looking forward to it."

Mr. Wilson stepped next to the truck and shook Mr. Barlow's hand.

"It's the least I can do for your helping me save the chicks."

Mr. Barlow pulled himself into the truck, started it up, and told Mr. Wilson he would call him about the owls in order to set up a time for their return.

Brianna was so excited about feeding the babies that she couldn't sit still. She tried to talk to Joey, but he was in the window seat now enjoying the view as they headed back home along the coast.

***

Thinking hard about the survival of the owlets, Brianna wondered how Mr. Barlow planned to save them. She worried about the chicks starving, but she had to trust Mr. Barlow. He said he would do his best, and she knew that was enough.

"What do they eat?" she asked.

He looked out at the rows of redwood trees before responding. "Feeding baby chicks is a little tricky. They eat all of an animal's parts, especially the bones for the calcium, and then they cough out the undigested parts, like the fur, bones, and tail."

Brianna had heard that touching a baby bird would make its parents reject it, but Mr. Barlow said that was a myth. "Most birds have a weak sense of smell," he continued. "They use their sight and hearing. Like all predators, the barn owls have special skills to help them hunt. For example, barn owls depend on their hearing to locate their prey. They can hear the quiet scurrying or rustling of small animals on the ground, sounds our ears couldn't hear."

Brianna loved animals as much as Mr. Barlow. "Do you think the babies will be re-united with their parents?" she asked.

"If we do everything according to what the birds understand instinctively, then they have a good chance. I'm going to build a big nesting box designed to keep the owlets safe, but it will also allow the parents to land on the edge and feed them. I don't want the babies falling out of the nest. They have no balance or awareness of danger, so the box needs to be deep but not too deep for the parents to feed all of them." Mr. Barlow glanced over at Joey and Brianna.

"Seven is a big family. Joey, can you picture yourself grabbing food off of your brother's plate to feed yourself? That's what animals and birds do instinctively to survive."

Brianna pictured the smallest owlet trying to compete for food. Her heart went out to him.

"I only take cookies from my baby brother's plate when he's not looking," Joey said.

"Joey, you're taking food out of your brother's mouth?" Brianna shook her head and rolled her eyes. "That is so uncool!"

"Hey, he doesn't even know it's gone. I eat it so fast he doesn't even know it was there. And then Mom gives him another cookie anyway."

Frowning, Brianna looked at Mr. Barlow's face, but he seemed to be smiling a little. She thought that if she had a little brother or sister, she would never steal their food. She wondered how much the baby barn owls would eat, and if they knew when they were full. They were almost home, and she hoped the babies weren't cold from their long trip.

***

Joey and Brianna watched Mr. Barlow gently carry the owlets' box to his garage. His long work bench had plenty of space for it. Opening the lid slowly, Mr. Barlow checked to see that each owlet had survived the trip. The littlest one was still and quiet. Brianna looked anxiously into Mr. Barlow's face, but he didn't appear concerned. Once he closed the lid, the screeching and hissing softened and almost stopped.

"I need to call my friend at the bird sanctuary and ask for her help. Why don't you both go home and then you can look up information about barn owls for me. We can meet later this afternoon. I may have to go food shopping for our friends here."

With a last glance at the precious box, Brianna and Joey turned away and left Mr. Barlow talking on the phone to Julie, the wild bird expert. Feeling sad and worried, Brianna wanted to stay with the owlets, but she didn't know what to do. She understood that she needed to learn about these birds before she could help them.

***

After saying goodbye to Joey, Brianna rushed to her room. She lived right next door to Mr. Barlow. He had taught her so much about animal behavior; she was eager to learn what she could and share it with him. She could be the bird tamer.

Brianna excitedly read page after page of information about the barn owls. She learned that their hearing was so good they could detect the heartbeat of a mouse from their perch. One ear is higher than the other. And their flat faces act like a satellite dish that triangulates sound to the ears so they can target prey. Their features work together to make the perfect homing device. Hunting at night, they eat small rodents. One owlet is born every two to three days, and the younger ones are smaller. Brianna thought of the littlest owl and felt badly for him because he would starve if he wasn't strong enough to compete with his siblings. Thinking she could save him, Brianna read more and more and decided that she would need to perform an owlet rescue. She would need to find a way to smuggle the littlest owl out of the box and bring it home where she could feed it the six mice it needed per day.

Ugh! Touch a live mouse? she thought.

Using her cell phone, Brianna looked up the closest pet store to her house. If she could ride Joey's bike, she could make a trip every day to buy the mice alive. She had earned his bike in a bet. Joey had given it to her after she had proven to him that she could tame cats like Mr. Barlow.

Now she would tame an owl.

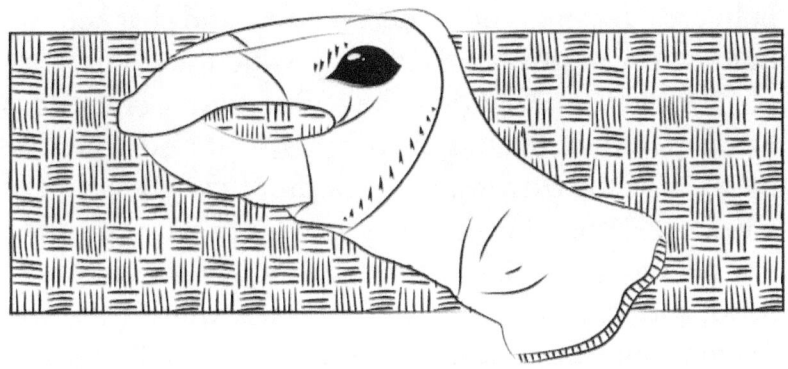

CHAPTER THREE

"Mom!"

"Yes, Brianna!"

"I'm going over to Mr. Barlow's, and I might be home around six. Is that OK?"

"Yes, we'll eat at 6:30 sharp."

Excited by all the knowledge she had learned about the owls, Brianna ran up the driveway and pushed the front doorbell. No one answered, so she knocked on the door to the garage.

The door opened, and Mr. Barlow's head appeared with his finger in front of his mouth to signal for her to be quiet. "The owls have settled down," he whispered. "I don't want them to start screeching again." He motioned Brianna over to the box on the table.

The light from the door made a thin path for her to see. With careful attention, Mr. Barlow lifted a flap, and she saw the big closed eyes and skinny, downy bodies of the chicks. They looked so small and helpless. Brianna held her breath and backed up quietly to wait for Mr. Barlow outside the door.

"I called my friend at the Wilderness Center who has experience feeding wild birds," he said when he met her in the driveway. "I told her how young these chicks are, and she said they need a good diet to get strong and grow. The chicks will fight for each bit of food, and the ones who are successful will mature and make it out of the nest."

"What about the weak ones? What happens to them, especially the tiny bloody one with his eyes closed?"

"He's still alive, but he's resting. I fed the other chicks, and they were quite aggressive. They pulled the meat right from my glove and kept gulping."

"Why did you use a glove?"

"You can't feed wild birds from your hand or close by because they imprint on you, or start to see you as their parents, especially with eye contact." He pulled a glove from his back pocket. "See, I painted an owl face on it to make it look like a bird, and I used my thumb and fingers like a beak." Mr. Barlow put on the glove, stretched out his hand, and opened and closed the thumb and top fingers.

Brianna took a closer look. She liked the face of the painted parent owl. Mr. Barlow had sewn the four fingers together to paint a big eye and beak. It looked pretty real.

"What did you feed them?" Briana imagined Mr. Barlow cutting up the heads and bodies of the mice to feed them the smaller pieces they could swallow. *Ugh!*

"My friend Julie at the wildlife center said I only need to feed the babies a meat, like ground beef, and mix in calcium. Once the parents find the babies in their new nesting box, they'll take over and feed them their proper diet. It's a special process where the acid in the owl's stomach helps it to digest and then spit out a 'pellet,' which is not digested. I've seen these pellets on the ground under the trees where our local owls have been feasting. Have you ever seen one?"

"I think I have. I found it on the ground below the big oak tree you call The Queen. It was like a gray ball with parts of fur and little bones stuck together. It was gross! But I saved it and put it in my collection."

For years Brianna had been collecting rocks, leaves, seeds, dried flowers, and everything she found in nature that would fit in her special boxes under her bed. Worried that she couldn't keep one of the owlets, she asked Mr. Barlow when he would be returning the babies to their nest. She needed an opportunity to convince him that she could keep one as a pet. The littlest one wouldn't survive with all his big brothers and sisters snatching his food.

"Can I feed the babies, Mr. Barlow? I feed Kitty Girl and she trusts me."

"A cat is not like a wild bird, Brianna. Kitty Girl was abandoned by people, but she had known humans and was familiar with them, even if they did mistreat her. A wild bird cannot be friends with a human. The glove I wear keeps my human-ness away from the chicks. They don't see my face, I don't speak to them, and they don't focus on me. They bond with whoever feeds them. I made the glove to look like a bird to imitate the parent."

Brianna and Mr. Barlow looked into the owlet box before he closed the flaps. "I'll have their new nest built tomorrow and then return the chicks in the late afternoon. You can come with me if you want to, but I don't want you to be sad. They need their parents, and it's the right thing to do. Wild predators like owls are only raised in captivity if they're so badly injured they can't fend for themselves in the wild."

"But, the littlest one—I named him Kita—he's too weak to eat!"

"Right now, he's resting to get stronger so he can eat. Don't give up on him, Brianna. Sometimes the smallest become the strongest."

"OK, I'll be patient. I need to go home and eat dinner, but I'll see you tomorrow after I finish my chores, OK? I want to go with you to return the babies to their parents."

"That's fine; I'll wait for you."

CHAPTER FOUR

Brianna was relieved she didn't need to feed all the babies herself, but Kita was special. He needed extra care. He looked so small and helpless in the box, especially since he had a little blood on his head. She couldn't imagine how he could even hold up his head to open his beak for food. Brianna decided to come back to the babies after dinner and feed Kita herself. She could take him out of the box, away from his siblings, and give him some food. That way, she was sure he would eat and gain strength. As she thought about it, she became more and more excited that she was doing a good deed and rescuing a helpless animal. She opened the back door with a slam. She was going to save Kita!

***

After finishing her dinner, Brianna went to her room and created a plan to save Kita. It would involve sneaking and being dishonest, but Brianna was touched by the desire to help a creature, a small injured creature that could not help itself and did not have protection from its parents. Brianna couldn't imagine what it must be like to be cold, alone, and hurt. She felt very secure in her family and did not have to compete for food! Stuffing a towel into her backpack, Brianna tiptoed into the kitchen to make Kita his late dinner.

Brianna located a small package of hamburger meat in the refrigerator. She opened the package and formed the meat into small balls the size of the pellet she had found. Then she ground several of her mom's calcium pills into a dust. She cut the pellets in half, scooped the white dust into the meat, and then patted it to form a ball again. Brianna placed the perfect balls in a plastic bag and hid them in her backpack. She listened for any sounds in the house. She closed the back door behind her softly.

Sneaking into Mr. Barlow's garage would be easy. He never locked the side door. Suddenly a pang of guilt flooded over her. Aware that she was a traitor, she remembered all the nice things that he had taught her and given her. She loved and appreciated animals so much more, and he was a friend who was so kind and helpful. He had even helped Joey to stop judging people before getting to know them. She, Joey, and Mr. Barlow had made lots of beautiful homes for the birds so they could nest. The three of them had formed a close tie while helping wildlife. They would stick the poles in the ground and mount the birdhouses that they hoped the birds would accept as their new homes. Brianna liked welcoming the new parents who were ready to hatch their babies. And the parents loved the birdhouses! Each spring every birdhouse was filled with loud chirping and baby beaks. Brianna could watch the babies eat all day long. What a job feeding all those mouths!

Inside her heart, Brianna knew that betraying Mr. Barlow was wrong, and she did not wish to hurt him. But the little drooping head of the chick and the noise and pushing bodies of the bigger chicks pulled her heart toward her owlet, Kita. She would have her own baby bird to keep warm and feed and grow to adulthood. Kita would change from a small bundle of downy fluff into a towering bird of prey with feathers of gold and black and white. The image stirred her imagination. They would be best friends, and she could teach him how to fly and hunt for himself. He might be a father, and she could help to raise his chicks. Brianna smiled at the idea of her own family whom she could love and care for.

***

With the light from her cell phone, Brianna made her way to Mr. Barlow's fence and crawled over it. She opened the side door to the garage slowly to avoid any creaking noises. She kept the light down and tiptoed over to the box. The chicks were silent, and the room was very dark. She didn't want to startle the owlets, so she placed her phone on a distant shelf and prepared to open the box flap.

"Brianna! What are you doing?"

Startled, she opened her mouth to scream and then remembered the chicks. Her hand flew to her lips.

"Oh my gosh! You scared me so badly!"

"I hope so, young lady! I don't want you to do anything to disturb the chicks."

But it was too late. Mr. Barlow's voice had excited them. Since nighttime was their natural hunting time, they were ready to be active and to search for food. Loud screeching filled the room, and Brianna stepped back, holding her head down so she didn't have to look at the disapproval on her friend's face.

"Did you come in here to feed the chicks?"

Brianna nodded her head.

"I am disappointed in you," he said. "Not trusting what I told you about the chicks is not what friends do. I thought I made it clear that humans can't feed them, because the chicks make a connection with you. Feeding them makes you their parent automatically. It disrupts the laws of nature and may endanger the chicks."

"I'm really, really sorry. I know that you told me that wild birds cannot be friends with humans, but the little one, Kita, needs more than a friend. He needs someone to take care of him and make sure he eats."

"Well, let's take a look and see how he's doing." He opened the top lid of the box and pointed his flashlight into the corner so as not to blind the chicks. All of them started hissing and rocking back and forth—even Kita held up his little head and opened his beak! Brianna almost cried out loud when she saw he was feeling stronger.

"Nature must take its course. We have to trust in survival of the fittest, even though we are compassionate and want to rescue every injured creature we see."

Brianna nodded her head in acknowledgement of what Mr. Barlow had told her.

"I know how you feel about animals and how we take care of them. Brianna, do you remember my mentioning my friend Julie?"

She nodded.

"Julie works at the Soberanes Wilderness Release Park where baby condors are raised and then released into the wild. All types of injured wild birds are cared for there, but the rangers use blinds or puppets to feed the birds so they don't imprint. If they imprint and see you as the food provider, then their independence is gone. People do make wonderful connections with all kinds of birds, but wild birds must be treated specially."

Looking into Mr. Barlow's kind eyes, Brianna understood that he knew she wanted to love and take care of a pet of her own.

"I understand. These barn owls are not pets."

Suddenly Brianna understood that her friendship with Mr. Barlow was more important than a relationship with any animal. She should not have doubted his knowledge about the birds. They were completely wild and did not need humans to take care of them, unless, of course, they were seriously injured and couldn't feed themselves.

"Can we visit the Wilderness Park? I'd love to go."

He carefully closed the lid of the box and turned toward her.

"I think you would enjoy seeing firsthand how professionals care for wild birds. Kita is feeling better, and soon you'll understand the importance of keeping wild things wild."

Mr. Barlow smiled and put his hand flat on the top of the box to be sure it was tightly closed and dark inside. Then they quietly left as the chicks settled down and rested for the night.

CHAPTER FIVE

The drive to the Wild Bird Center at Soberanes Wilderness Park was exciting. Brianna looked down the steep cliffs to see the vast blue ocean and the wind whipping the water, sending spray leaping high above the rocks.

"How do the condors live here, Mr. Barlow?" Brianna asked.

"They depend on watching other scavengers finding the dead animals. The thermals, or air above the water, provide a kind of highway for their exploration. It's exciting to see their wing spans. They can be twelve feet wide, more than the length of my truck." He looked over at Brianna. "I don't know if they will have adults to release back into the wild when we visit today, but I'm sure they have young birds we can see. The center has a unique way of feeding the chicks and young adults with no human contact."

Puzzled, Brianna asked, "But why is it so important that the chicks don't think that humans are their parents? We take care of lots of animals: sheep, cows, chickens, goats."

"Those animals are used as a food source. We don't eat wild birds. Keeping them wild is the best way to protect them. Living around humans makes the birds trust humans, and not all people can be trusted around these birds."

"Why not? I would take very good care of Kita and make him part of our family."

"Brianna, you are a kind and loving person. Not all people are kind and loving to birds and animals." Mr. Barlow turned his truck onto a dirt road. "Here we are!"

They parked, and Brianna followed Mr. Barlow up to a small building.

A smiling young woman in brown pants and brown shirt answered the door. "Hello there!" She held out her hand. "Welcome to the Soberanes Wilderness Park. You must be Brianna. I was expecting you. We're going on a tour together. My name is Julie."

Brianna smiled and shook the guide's hand. "Hi, Julie. We're here to see the baby condor chicks and learn about your preserve." Brianna kept shaking the lady's hand because she was so excited.

Laughing, Julie replied, "Well, let's not waste a minute."

She took a second to say hello to Mr. Barlow. "Follow me," she said, turning back to Brianna. "I'll show you the young adults' aviary. You understand that California condors are an endangered species, right, Brianna?"

"Oh, yes, Julie. You're raising the chicks to become adults and then releasing them back into the wild because there are so few of them surviving."

"That's right. We take them from the nest when they're about four to six months old and place them in large pens so we can 'puppet feed' them until they can feed themselves. Then we move them to the young adult aviary, which is extremely large, so the birds can learn to fly and yet still be protected."

Julie led Brianna to a tall fence that was covered by a thin net, and Mr. Barlow followed behind. Trees and bushes and tall grasses grew everywhere. Brianna didn't see any condors, but she thought they might be night birds like her owls.

"Do they hunt at night, Julie?

"No, we feed them and study them with what's called a blind. That way, the wild birds don't see or hear humans. They just fly to the feeding area and eat. It's not difficult to feed them, because the condors eat only dead animals, so they feed during the day. We don't have any chicks here right now, but we can hide behind the blind and observe the young adult. Step over here."

Julie added, "Some release-parks use a hand puppet made to look like a condor to feed younger chicks who aren't ready to fly yet."

"Mr. Barlow uses a glove to feed our baby chicks!"

Julie smiled. "The state of California is very serious about strengthening this bird population. Our condors are an important part of the food chain." Brianna nodded her head; she had learned about ecosystems and food chains in school.

"What do you know about baby barn owls, Julie?" Brianna asked.

"Very few come into our preserve, Brianna. They hunt inland, and people make them into pets if they're injured, so we release the ones we do feed just as we do the condors. We release the mice into the blind if the owls are flying and feed them with hand puppets if they're fledglings."

"Can I watch the condor eat, Julie?" She was curious to see a real condor. "I see a lot of turkey vultures near my house, but I've never seen a condor."

"Well, you're in luck; our condor should be flying overhead soon. Let's be quiet and see if he is hungry."

They tiptoed into what seemed like an enclosure of green vines and thick brush. Julie motioned her to a small gap where she could be hidden and yet see into an open space. Brianna moved closer and peered through the space. She saw what looked like a deer lying down. Brianna pulled back in shock and looked at Mr. Barlow's face. Sensing her panic, he motioned to Julie and they backed away slowly from the wall of thick green foliage. Following Julie's lead, Brianna stepped quickly and soon found herself in front of the cabin where Julie had greeted her.

Mr. Barlow looked directly into Brianna's eyes. "I'm sorry. I thought you understood that the condors feed on dead animals. It's so important to the food cycle. All of the rotting meat is, in a way, cleaned up and, at the same time, it provides these birds with food. Bacteria and other pathogens are kept away from the healthy side of nature. We need these birds to remove the diseased parts of our environment. They're like nature's cleaning crew."

"But it was a big deer! It may have been a mother!"

"Yes, but the deer die of natural causes, just like the sheep, cows, and other large animals the condors feed on. They even feed on the bodies of whales!"

Brianna looked at Julie who smiled.

"I agree with Mr. Barlow. We need the condors, and our center does not kill animals for the condors to eat. The local ranchers and various departments who remove dead animals provide the carcasses so that the condors can survive."

After Brianna and Mr. Barlow thanked Julie for her time, Brianna looked out the window of the truck and imagined she was a condor.

Sailing with open wings on the winds of the
water, a disturbance below catches her eye. She
circles lower and lower until she digs her talons
into the earth. She steps forward with her
friends and tears pieces for herself.

"We all need to get our food from some source, right Mr. Barlow?" I am not so different from the condors, she thought. I need to eat.

Mr. Barlow started the truck. "We are so fortunate, that we have so many different kinds of food. Our little barn owls are created just for keeping the small rodent population in check. We have the freedom to enjoy salads, pizza, ice cream, and so many delicious choices. Let's go home and build a home for the owlets so they can eat a good dinner with their folks."

CHAPTER SIX

As Mr. Barlow drove his truck under the overhanging branches of the redwood trees, Brianna asked him if he had seen the movie, *The Lion King*.

"I think it was an animal film, wasn't it?"

"Yes. Our barn owls remind me of lions a little bit. We're helping our baby owls return to the circle of life! The owlets are coming home."

"That's right!" Mr. Barlow turned into his driveway. "Give Joey a call so he can help us build the owl box."

Brianna got out of the truck. "Can I check on the baby chicks first?"

"Of course, but wait for me because I'll feed them while you're here."

Brianna waited for Mr. Barlow at the door to the garage. He returned from his house with a bag and a glove. She noticed that in the bag he had substituted mouse parts for the hamburger and calcium he had fed them at first. Opening the door slowly, the two quietly stepped into the garage.

As soon as Mr. Barlow opened the top flaps of the box, the screeching and hissing started, and little fuzzy heads bobbed up and down.

"Wow, they must be really hungry!" she exclaimed.

Mr. Barlow pulled on his leather glove with the fingers sewn together and the thumb painted like a beak. The sides of the glove looked like an adult owl with large eyes. Brianna laughed at the "mother" owl with meat in her beak. The biggest baby jumped, grabbed a piece, and quickly gulped it down.

Brianna watched in fascination as Mr. Barlow repeated the motion, and soon all the meat was gone. Happy that the littlest, Kita, had several chunks all to himself, she relaxed and smiled. Soon the babies would be reunited with their parents and their feeding would be natural.

"I'm going to call Joey now, Mr. Barlow."

Taking off the glove, Mr. Barlow agreed to meet Joey and Brianna after lunch in his wood shop.

Mr. Barlow left the garage first. Brianna moved closer to the closed box and put her hand on the side where Kita sat. She whispered a sad goodbye to the beautiful little baby that she had hoped to love. "Maybe you'll remember us, Kita. I'm so glad you're going back to nature. Please don't forget us and how we tried our best to be good parents to you, if only for a little while." She imagined that Kita was closing his eyes and falling into a gentle sleep. She tiptoed out of the room and quietly closed the door.

***

Singing her favorite song, Brianna turned up Mr. Barlow's driveway once again and looked for Kitty Girl.

Nowhere in sight, Brianna thought. She's being mysterious.

A loud machine made a buzzing sound, and she knew Mr. Barlow was in his wood shop. As she walked through the open door, she saw him pushing a long piece of wood through the saw. When he was finished cutting, Mr. Barlow turned off the saw and smiled at Brianna.

"Did you call Joey?

"Yes, he's coming over after he finishes his chores. He's excited about making an owl box."

While Mr. Barlow cut more wood, Joey stepped into the shop with Kitty Girl in his arms. Suddenly she jumped down and raced out.

Mr. Barlow laughed. "I'm afraid Kitty Girl doesn't like the sound of machines. She isn't used to it, so she's scared of it."

"I know," Joey bragged. "It's the old fight or flight idea, right?"

"That's right, and that's true for all of us. There's a little bit of wild animal in all of us."

Joey laughed and made growling sounds. Brianna smiled at Joey's display of his wild animal powers.

Brianna and Joey looked at all the pieces of wood set out on the table. Brianna couldn't imagine how Mr. Barlow was going to put the pieces together to make a special home for the owls. "How do you know how to build this owl box?" she asked.

"I searched on the internet for a professional who makes barn owl boxes for a living. He has built thousands of these boxes and explains all of his ideas. He also sells them because barn owls can be helpful in keeping the mice population away from grain and feed for animals. That's why they're called barn owls. They hunt and nest near barns where mice are happy to eat all of a rancher's grain for his horses and cattle."

Mr. Barlow held up two flat sides of the box together to make a corner. "The box needs to be a certain size for comfort. This one will be 23 inches wide, 16 inches tall, and 13 inches deep. It will be crowded, but the owls don't mind. To protect against predators like raccoons attacking the babies, I'm making a divider inside the box. The opening will be an oval, which is the shape of the owls, and not their most dangerous enemy, the great horned owl. I'm not going to paint it, because paint creates heat. We'll use a good, strong wood to make the box. It's going to weigh about 23 pounds, which is not that light."

Mr. Barlow instructed Joey on how to use the vices to hold the wood pieces tightly so they could be sanded. Then Mr. Barlow started Brianna with gluing the wood pieces, and soon they were assembled. She enjoyed the smell of the wood and the camaraderie of making a project together. She was surprised Joey was so intense and focused on his part. Usually, he was making jokes and being silly.

"OK, I think we're almost finished," Mr. Barlow said. "Brianna, take handfuls of the wood shavings and put them in the box. Joey, you can paint the sealer on the wood. Then we're ready to go! I'm calling Mr. Wilson to let him know we're coming over with the box and to set up a ladder."

***

While Mr. Barlow was on the phone, Brianna ran over to the garage to check on the chicks. She was worried that they would not enjoy the transition to their new home.

When Mr. Barlow opened the garage door to get the chicks for the ride back to the ranch, she asked him, "Who will take care of seven little helpless hungry chicks if the parents reject them?"

"We need to go one step at a time and hope for the best. The babies have only been gone for just over a day, so the parents would still be looking for them. Mr. Wilson has spotted the parents flying over the dead branch. That is a very good sign. They haven't left the area and deserted their chicks."

Brianna felt relieved that the parents were so attached to their babies. She wanted the owlets to grow up to be big and strong and beautiful, especially Kita. His big, black, innocent eyes and curious look were deep in her heart. He was special, and she knew how important he was in keeping down the mouse population and to balance nature.

***

With the new owl box safely secured in the truck bed, Brianna and Joey peacefully shared the front seat and stared out the window. Mr. Barlow started up his engine and moved onto the highway. Seven homeless chicks would soon be reunited with their parents, and they'd be lovingly taken care of. At least that's how Brianna saw it. She was a step-mom for a time and had thoroughly enjoyed herself.

"Are there more wood projects we can do with you, Mr. Barlow?" Joey asked.

"I can teach you all sorts of woodworking. We can make tables, chairs, boxes, bowls, and just about anything you want to. I would enjoy having apprentices to work with."

Joey smiled.

Soon they were stopping at Mr. Wilson's gate, with the sign swaying in the wind. After they were through, Mr. Barlow closed the gate behind them and pulled himself back into the truck. He let out a laugh. "I miss the life of a rancher, the wildlife, and the hard work. It is a beautiful property. I wish I could own it."

Brianna admired the green, rolling open spaces dotted with big trees of different varieties. She and Joey watched the horses and cattle in the pastures and the goats, ducks, and chickens searching for the best tidbits. Brianna wasn't afraid of hard work. She thought of herding the horses on a sure-footed quarter horse and imagined all the beautiful manes and tails flowing in the wind as they raced across the meadows.

Mr. Barlow stopped near the house, and Mr. Wilson walked up to the idling truck to direct him where to park. The owl box was heavy, so they needed to park close to the oak tree.

"Once these owlets fledge and leave the box, John, I'm going to take down this old tree. I know many birds have enjoyed its comfort and safety, but a wind will knock it down, and then it's not useful to anyone anymore."

"You're right," Mr. Barlow said. "Nature lets us know when it's time to move on."

Brianna sensed his gaze on her. She looked into his eyes and saw a bit of sadness, but a bit of hope too.

Mr. Barlow carefully lifted the owl box out of the truck bed. Two men who worked on the ranch positioned a ladder next to the stump of the dead branch. Just that small part of the branch would hold the box next to the trunk. Suddenly, two dark shadows filled the sky, and everyone looked up to see. Two big barn owls circled and then dove down as if to attack the ladder. Everyone stepped back.

"Be careful, John." Mr. Wilson said. "You could be attacked when you secure the owl box to the stump."

Mr. Barlow took in a breath. "I'm ready to do what I can." Holding the owl box under his left arm, he grabbed the rungs of the ladder as the two men held it steady. Very slowly, he climbed all the way to the broken branch. He wedged the owl box into the fork made by the branch stump and the trunk. Brianna held her breath as she watched him secure the box to the tree with a strong rope. She smiled. Mr. Barlow was the best, and the box would hold all seven of the chicks and the parents.

Mr. Barlow stepped down the ladder carefully. He was a big man and could easily fall if he was careless.

"Look at your face, Brianna," he said in a kind way. "Don't hold your breath! Everything is OK. The new nest box is secured, and now we're ready to place the chicks in there."

She looked at the cardboard box in the truck bed and then back at Mr. Barlow. "Just be careful, OK. We need our cat tamer and barn owl tamer."

He smiled. "I'm ready for the big test!" Mr. Barlow announced.

Mr. Wilson's two ranch hands grabbed the ladder tightly to secure it. Mr. Barlow carefully lifted the box of chicks, and Brianna made a silent wish that the parents would accept their babies. They had flown away at the noise of talking and the movement, but Mr. Barlow had impressed upon her how strong the bond was between parents and babies. He pulled the box closer to his chest. Then he removed gloves from his back pocket so that the chicks would not peck him when he lifted each one into the box. Their beaks were small, but Brianna knew how strong wild animals and birds can be when they're frightened.

"OK," Mr. Barlow said to the ranch hands, "make sure that you hold onto that ladder, even if the parents attack me. I expect them to protect the place where they last fed their babies. I don't think they'll touch me, but their actions will scare most predators away."

Joey gave Brianna a concerned look. She reached out and touched his arm to reassure him. All the time that the three of them had shared together showed in their faces. All three smiled at each other and crossed their fingers. If nature was kind, this owl family would be reunited soon.

Mr. Barlow took his time grabbing each ladder rung and lifting each foot. Then he faced the box and adjusted his weight. The chicks didn't make a sound until Mr. Barlow opened the box flaps. Loud hissing and screeching filled the air as he slowly lifted each chick into the owl box. Maintaining his balance, he ignored the chicks' head and talon movement, even though his head was straight in the path of fourteen large extended claws aiming for his eyes. The parents flew closer and closer to him in circles, but he never looked up or ducked his head in fear. The last chick disappeared safely into the box, and the parents flew away after circling several times. Mr. Barlow carefully descended the ladder and wiped the sweat from his brow. He smiled at everyone, and they clapped in acknowledgement of his bravery. Two angry wild birds with talons that could seriously injure him were gone. But would they return? The chicks kept up their noise, and everyone waited in suspense.

Brianna held her breath again, but Mr. Barlow smiled at her and showed her his crossed fingers. She let the air out of her lungs and held up her own crossed fingers. Mr. Wilson and Joey laughed and did the same. The ranch hands carried away the ladder, and everyone moved back from the tree. Some of the branches still had dark green oak leaves pushing out like small bunches of berries at the end of long, spindly branches. These native oaks were tough and ageless. Almost.

After what seemed like forever, two small specks appeared to their left. Flying over the open meadow, the barn owls swooped down once more, but this time they landed on a strong branch above the owl box. The smaller bird flew off, but she made a slow circle and found the edge where she could land. Suddenly the babies started screeching louder.

It was as if she were asking the chicks, *Where have you been?* They were very excited to see their mom!

Everyone starting talking at once, which seemed to frighten the parents, but after they flew away, they returned. A great feeling of success and pride filled Brianna. It was a wonderful thing to be able to help birds and animals survive when they had been threatened by death. Brianna thought of Julie and how much she must love her job helping all the condors and watching them fly away once they were released to the freedom they understood. Maybe I should help animals as a career, thought Brianna. Nothing had made her feel as good as when she was petting Kitty Girl or watching Mr. Barlow feed the owlets.

CHAPTER SEVEN

"Are you ready for a fun ride, Brianna and Joey?" yelled Mr. Wilson. "You too, John!" Walking back to the buildings, he stopped near a shed where he flung open the door. There stood two ATVs, the answer to easier, faster transportation on large ranches.

Joey ran to the closest one and touched the big tire. Four big tires surrounded an open metal cage with two seats. Brianna thought they looked like small jeeps with the sides open. A bright green plastic shell covered the rear motor and the front section.

Brianna ran over to the other ATV, climbed onto the passenger seat, and pulled the half door shut. As she tugged the seat belt tight against her body, Brianna looked around at the frame of thick bars that surrounded her. Mr. Wilson handed her a helmet, and she felt even safer.

After the helmets were adjusted for all the riders, Mr. Wilson turned toward the others and said, "Are you ready to see the ranch and watch our cowboys move some cattle?"

Joey grinned at Mr. Wilson and waved his arms. "Let's go!" he shouted.

Mr. Barlow smiled at Brianna and got into the driver's seat. "I haven't been a gardener all my life, Brianna," he explained to her. "I worked every summer at the Wilson's ranch when I was in school. I rode horses, cut trees, camped under the stars, and learned a lot about nature. It wasn't until I married and settled down that I stayed at one job." He adjusted his seat belt. "Is yours secure?" he asked. Brianna tugged on her own latch to show that it was.

Mr. Barlow looked over at Joey and Mr. Wilson in their ATV and yelled, "Are we set to go?"

Both engines roared. Brianna thought the cattle would quickly run away once they heard these giant bees. "Hold on to the bar to your right, Brianna," Mr. Barlow shouted, and they were off!

The little open cars bumped over the ground and moved quickly in the open spaces. Mr. Wilson took the lead, and Brianna could hear Joey yelling "whoopee" as they bounced. In every direction, the ranchland stretched around them with covered hills and oak forests. The wide tires of Joey's ATV kicked up dust, obscuring Brianna's view until Mr. Barlow slowed down and put a little distance between the vehicles.

✻✻✻

Hanging on tightly to her roll cage bar, Brianna admired the open rolling hills and thought of long ago when buffalo herds filled the pastures. She had never seen so much open space. Galloping a horse on these meadows would be a joy. She imagined she was racing on a pony for miles and miles.

Up ahead Brianna could see a real buffalo herd. No, they were large black cows with big ears grazing in the tall grass. Yes, they were the cows Mr. Wilson called beef cattle, which meant they were raised to be eaten. She thought of the condors and the barn owls doing their part to contribute to nature.

Everyone seems to have a purpose, she thought and smiled.

Mr. Wilson stopped his ATV and waited for Mr. Barlow and Brianna to pull up beside them. He signaled for Mr. Barlow to turn off his engine. With the engines silent, Brianna could hear Mr. Wilson explain that they would follow the cowboys who would direct the cattle to the barns. Suddenly Brianna heard the pounding of hooves on the ground. Three men on running horses appeared to their left, moving swiftly toward the herd. One cowboy called loudly and swung his arm with a rope over his head. Then he leaned down, spurred his horse, and ran right past the startled animals who looked up in alarm. Hearing the other cowboys yelling behind them and rushing about, several of the cows started running and followed the cowboy who appeared to lead.

Soon the entire herd was running, and the thrill of the ground pounding made Brianna imagine she was racing with the animals. Mr. Wilson and Mr. Barlow started the ATVs and shot forward so they were chasing the cowboys and the herd in one long parade. The cowboys whooped and yelled, and soon everyone was whooping and yelling, joining in the fun of racing in the wind. Faster and faster they rode, until the cowboys turned the herd away from the trees and down a long slope toward three large barns sitting in the middle of several corrals.

Brianna watched in amazement as the cowboys guided the herd until they slowed and walked into the opened gates, the cows huffing and puffing from their long run. Cowboys on the ground quickly shut the gates once the corrals were full, and soon a mass of bobbing black heads surrounded the three barns like bees on a honeycomb. Picking up speed, Mr. Wilson and Mr. Barlow turned their vehicles toward a wide road to return to the ranch house.

Brianna sat back and enjoyed the open freedom of the little car. She leaned forward to see Joey's face, and he seemed lost in the pure joy of the experience. She knew Joey loved to race on his bicycle and skateboard, but this was even better. The views of all the grass and trees and big bushes were special. One day she hoped to live in an open space with nature surrounding her—kind of like Mr. Barlow's place, but bigger.

As the ATVs stopped before the sheds, everyone unbuckled, pulled off their helmets, and ran together to share their favorite parts of the ride. Joey thought the cowboys were the best, and Brianna thought the horses were the best. She would never get over her love of horses. She had promised herself she would own her own when she found the money and the opportunity.

Mr. Wilson collected their helmets and invited the group into the house for a cold drink. Everyone smiled enthusiastically, and the four brushed the dust from their clothes before they went inside.

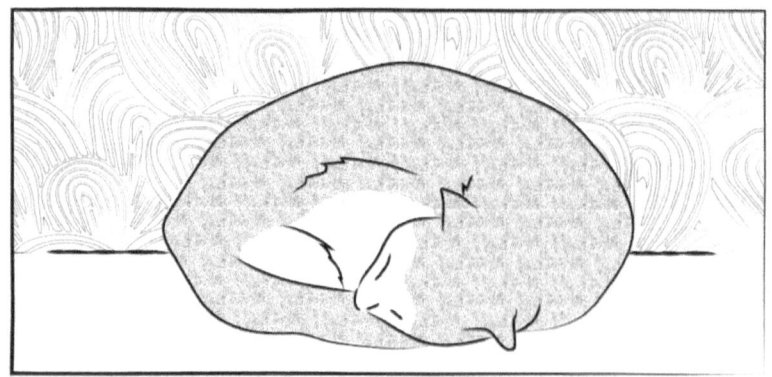

CHAPTER EIGHT

Joey and Brianna were quiet on the ride home, but Brianna was happy. What a day! Reuniting baby barn owls with their frantic parents, leaping over the ground like a running stag, and joining in a real roundup! No wonder no one was talking.

When Mr. Barlow pulled his truck in front of Joey's house, Joey hopped out and walked over to Mr. Barlow's window. "Thank you so much. Today was the best day of my life, and it's because of you. You've taught me a lot about friendship and kindness and even how to build things. I can't believe that I once thought you were a scary person who wanted to frighten people. You're the nicest person I've ever met. Please forgive me for being mean and stupid. I'll never be that person again."

Joey held out his hand for Mr. Barlow to shake, and they smiled at each other.

"You're welcome, Joey." Mr. Barlow reached out with his other hand and patted him on the shoulder.

Brianna thought about what Joey had said. He had really changed. But then again, she had changed, too, and she knew in her heart the meaning of the circle of life, a cycle of life and death and constant change.

She watched Mr. Barlow's face as they headed for his driveway. Before she jumped out of the truck, she asked him if they could talk for a little before she went home.

"Sure. Let's sit on the porch and see if Kitty Girl will join us."

Brianna remembered the day that she had first petted Kitty Girl. The cat had been sitting in Mr. Barlow's lap with a contented look on her face. She didn't run away or do anything strange when Brianna reached out her hand. Brianna thought she might be frightened of a new person in her life, but Mr. Barlow had convinced the animal that she was safe and secure. What a wonderful thing to give the world.

With just their private thoughts, they sat in their chairs on the porch, waiting for Kitty Girl to make her entrance. She was quite the lady and expected everyone to marvel at her beautiful tail and fur of black and white.

"Well, Brianna, what did you think of today?"

"I was so excited to return the chicks, sorry to lose Kita, happy the mom and dad were still looking for their chicks, and so glad you weren't hurt when you placed the box in the tree. You did a wonderful thing, and I understand now why we can't keep wild birds or animals for our pets."

"And why is that?"

"At the Wilderness Center, I saw that nature has its own plan. We're just kind of out there trying to understand and do our best with nature. I wanted Kita to be safe, but it was not my place to interfere. I understand that now. The dead deer upset me, but that's also nature's way. We all seem to have a wish to help whatever in nature needs help, like Kitty Girl, starving and scared. Like Kita, who was injured and helpless. But I could have made a big mess of things if I had fed Kita and made him my pet. He was a wild bird, and he didn't even know what I was. How could I have helped him if I didn't even know what he was—a wild bird! I read stuff on the internet, but those were just facts and things that told me how other people had acted. Seeing Kita in his condition with his brothers and sisters was different. You made me realize that I was not his family. He is a barn owl, and I am a human. How different could we be!"

Mr. Barlow leaned back in his chair and looked at her with a smile. "You were so loving and caring about Kita that you forgot that humans can play an important part in wildlife, but we are not necessarily the answer to the creatures' needs. We want to be helpful, and we do have the right intentions, but we have millions of years to learn. Barn owls and cats each have a history that we just enjoy today for what it is. We've learned a lot about their habits and food, and there are professional societies, organizations, and special places, like the Soberanes Wilderness Center, that give a helping hand to nature."

Brianna asked again, softly, "But what if the parents had not accepted the babies and rejected them?"

"Good question. Mr. Wilson's ranch hand, the one who had climbed the tree to make sure it was safe for me to use a ladder on the old oak, discovered that dead animal parts had been shoved into open spaces in the tree's trunk. It was obvious that the parents were trying to feed the babies, even though they weren't there. Can you imagine how strong an instinct these birds feel towards their young? Even though the babies were gone, the parents never abandoned their chicks. What a wonderful fact. We can all feel good about the way nature takes care of its own."

"Wow, I can't believe that I tried to interfere with the natural order of things. I am so grateful to you for understanding and knowing what these owlets needed."

"Brianna, you are my friend, and I knew that the first day that you spied on me that we were going to share fun adventures. Kitty Girl and the owlets are just the beginning of what we can do to help nature. I know how much you love animals and birds, and love is a good start. Now we can call the Soberanes Wilderness Center and do what we can to help them release the condors and other wild birds."

She looked at him, smiling, and said, "You're the best teacher I've ever had."

Unexpectedly, Kitty Girl jumped up into Brianna's lap and curled up for a good scratch.

THE END

ACKNOWLEDGMENTS

To my husband, Steve, who inspired this story and shares my love of nature.

To Jennifer Chesak for all her dedication and skill and support.

To Dale Egron, a knowledgeable bird lover and supporter of all wildlife.

To Emily Wikle for her creative talent and contribution.

To the Ventana Wildlife Society for their educational condor and conservation programs

To the following books:

Wesley the Owl by Stacey O'Brien

The Year of the Greylag Goose by Konrad Lorenz

ABOUT THE AUTHOR

Mary Busby describes herself as a nature lover. Her first book, *The Cat Tamer*, shows how gardens and animals give so much pleasure. This second book reaches out to nature by focusing on birds and the natural processes we humans need to respect. Falling in love with the beauty of California, Mary attended college here and graduated from Stanford University to teach English Literature in private schools for 25 years. Her devotion to the preservation of natural landscapes and forests is a life-long passion. From her enjoyment of Lake Park in Milwaukee, Wisconsin, to woodland hikes in Jacks Peak Park, Monterey, California, she says so often, "Nature never disappoints."

ABOUT THE ILLUSTRATOR

Emily Wikle is a graphic designer and fine artist based in Los Angeles, California. She graduated with degrees in studio arts and art history from the University of California, Davis in 2015 and currently works as a graphic design and marketing specialist for an international commercial real estate firm. In her work, Emily explores different ways to communicate visually at the intersection of her fine arts background and graphic design skills. By incorporating traditional methods into digital, she boosts her bold and clean designs with rich hand-drawn qualities. In her free time, Emily can be found hiking with her camera, creating album artwork for musicians, and testing out new recipes.